Burnt

Tim Kirk

Burnt by Tim Kirk

ISBN: 978-1-938349-27-0
eISBN: 978-1-938349-28-7
Library of Congress Control Number: 2015937341

"Burnt" was originally written as an online serial. Chapters were
published weekly between January 2010 and February 2011

Layout and Book Design by Mark Givens
Illustrations by Thomas Carroll

First Pelekinesis Printing 2015

For information:
Pelekinesis, 112 Harvard Ave #65, Claremont, CA 91711 USA

www.pelekinesis.com

Burnt

Tim Kirk

for Briar

WARING.

1873

The prairie goes on and on. Nothing moves. As if nothing has ever moved.

A sudden gust of wind rustles scrub and a dark shape appears, upright, cracking the bleak horizon right down the middle.

A rider on a horse.

Ahead is a squat adobe. In the doorway, a cigarette dies. Falling hooves grow closer. A sentry presses his back against the door, light from within shimmers around the brim of his hat.

A sharp intake of breath as a horse appears out of the dark night, stirrups bouncing below an empty saddle. He catches the reins with one hand; the other hand holds a gun.

He runs his fingers along the horse's flank. Wet with sweat.

Inside, a dozen men are frozen over a coffin, eyes on the door, hands hovering over their gun-belts. A beautiful young woman is laid out there, her arms cross her chest.

The sentry steps in. "Just a horse," he says, relighting his cigarette.

"The rider?" asks the largest of the large men.

The sentry blows smoke. "No rider."

The big man kicks the floor and a rifle is in his hands. He throws aside a man and then a door. In a small room, there is an empty cradle and an open window.

Curtains blow.

A horse whinnies.

The posse charges outside and fires blindly into the dark night.

WARING!

A vaquero crouches in the dry brush. He carefully lays his hat on the ground and raises his head. The stars are fading in the growing light of dawn. The camp is quiet. A smoldering fire. A saddle outside a simple lean-to. A horse stirs with a sleepy snort and a nicker.

The cowboy reaches for his hat. It's gone. A knife streaks across his neck.

Jeff Waring squats and watches. After a while, the thrashing and gurgling slows and then stops. Waring reaches over dripping twigs, the puddling blood and grabs a handful of shirt. He yanks the dead man upright.

He's not one of Arango's men. He's an independent operator. Probably just a horse thief.

The earth devours the blood. Relief flows over him. Waring looks at the camp. It's a peaceful scene. The baby lies swaddled in a horse blanket by his saddle. It starts to cry and he smiles.

"*My* baby."

There is a cleft in the rocky bluff. It's a natural fit for a baby and Waring slides her in there. He leans over the edge for a better look.

Down in the valley, the wagon train has given up on the circle. Arango stands in what's left of its center.

Arango should seem a dot at this distance, dwarfed by the immense desert and towering mesas. But he is no dot. Surrounded by all this, Arango is huge.

Vaqueros prod, they push and in this way a child is ushered forth. This is Eirik's son. Eirik helped Waring build a little hammock for the baby and his wife nursed her over fifty miles of dirt and rocks. Arango rests his pistol on the boy's forehead and fires.

The shot and the scream bounce around the canyon, around the wailing pioneers, around Waring and the baby.

Next up are Jokkum and Nina's twins.

Arango is turning in circles now, shouting at the surrounding hills. The shouts are too faint for Waring to understand, but he assumes Arango is repeating his threat — that he'll kill all the children in the wagon train if the baby is not returned.

The twins hold hands. Waring swaddles the baby in a blanket their mother knit as Arango fires twice.

The vaqueros are burning the wagons. Arango starts in on the older children.

Waring takes the baby in his arms and speaks quietly to her. "Do you see? The devil determines their order." He lifts the baby, giving her a better look at the carnage below. "Do you see? Do you see what this world is?"

He holds her face close to his. Her lids flutter. Her eyes focus. He starts to say, "Do you see what I am?"

No. That's for when she's older.

The old woman chokes it out between sobs. She tells him what he already knows. There are no men in Los Rios. They are with Arango. They are searching for the baby.

Waring lays his rifle across his saddle and waits as the women and children gather their things. He doesn't dismount. They don't have much.

He tries to remember the baby names. Martina had one for a boy and one for a girl. Then Arango saw her in the window of the farmhouse. Arango kidnapped his wife and, by doing so, also the baby inside her. It took Waring months to track them to Mexico. By the time he did, Martina was dead and he'd forgotten the names for their baby.

For a kick, he balances the girl on the horse's neck.

She bounces up and down as he leads the people of Los Rios into the desert.

When they stumble, he drives them on. When they collapse, he leaves them to die.

Riding back towards the border, he shows her an apple and a knife. She wheezes. He cuts the apple and presses a slice to her lips. The wheeze becomes a laugh.

She tugs at his mask. He tosses it over her. She luxuriates in the black silk.

They straggle into town from time to time. Angry men, weary of traveling, weary of being driven by their anger. And they all want to kill him.

Waring found this one behind Stabler's barn, passing a bottle with a couple of tough-looking hombres from Mex Town.

"I have a message for Arango. He ain't gonna like it."

The vaquero wears two guns. He rests his palms on them. "English not so good, *señor.*"

"In that case, I'll just give you the gist of it. It's mainly contempt. Contempt and scorn. We've been playing a game, him and me, and I'm winning. Arango took my woman and he took my child. But the woman died and I took the child back. He followed me and killed everyone in the wagon train I was traveling with. But I doubled-back and killed everyone in his damn village. I killed the women. I killed the children. Maybe I killed your woman? Maybe I killed your children?"

Now they both have their palms on their guns. "So run along now. Tell your boss what I told you."

The man is smiling and his English is a lot better. "*Señor*, I am not going anywhere."

"You won't give him my message in this world? Then go on and give it to him in the next."

And now it gets loud.

Over the years, Waring has learned to rock from side to side as he fires. So far, this has worked well for him. He gets hit less and the movement doesn't affect his shooting all that much.

This time is no different. He's unhurt and the other guy is dead. And since he has his gun out, he keeps shifting left and right and firing and takes out the rest of the fuckers.

It was shortly after this that the good town people of Rubio City, New Mexico made Jeff Waring their Sheriff.

The steady stream of settlers has meant hasty additions to Rubio City. A cemetery at one edge of town and a tent for birthing at the other. Undertakers stay put but doctors come and go so Waring mans the tent. He has his hands deep in the Jennings woman when Cooper makes his drunken entrance.

"Holy shit! Stafford wasn't pulling my leg at all! It's Jeff Waring in the flesh."

He offers a bottle. Waring shows him his bloody hands.

"Finish her up quick and I'll buy ya a drink. The whole gang is over there – Stafford, Nichols and Dakota. That's what Martin's going by these days."

"Not the Dakota *Kid*?"

Cooper laughs his familiar open-mouthed laugh. Waring peers into it, seeing every drunken night with this gang, every filthy saloon, every imagined offense, every unwarranted brawl and knife-fight. He tastes the liquor, smells the sawdust, feels the horror of waking to a snoring whore and an aching pecker.

"*Sheriff* Waring! Who would have thought it?!"

He pictures a tree with four nooses. Better yet, he sees a sturdy gallows that can handle four. He can imagine just how he'll build it. The design appears in his mind, fully conceived.

With a wail, the child enters this rotten world. It's a boy.

.C L A Y.

1923

A laundry truck pitches madly through the forest. Tires rock the rutted road, crashing into and laboring out of deep puddles. Water flows in an undisturbed sheet down the windshield.

The driver squints. A yellow slicker swims into view. A horrid squeal of mud-coated brakes as the driver tears off his own coat. He tosses it atop a bundle on the seat next to him.

But there is no need. The man in the slicker waves him on. Another man gestures towards a space between two larger trucks.

He chokes out the engine. Fog clouds the glass. He unstraps the canvas door and peels it back. The truck on his left has something painted on the side – it's a camera on a tripod. Someone inside shouts over the rain. "Betcha we're not rolling until this lets up?"

"I betcha right."

"Enjoy your day off."

He straps up the canvas and the fog reappears. He picks up the baby. The plan had been to ditch the truck somewhere and find a dry rock to sleep under. Not much of a plan. Maybe this is better.

A burst of lightning reveals a clearing in the dark woods. He's part of a camp of two dozen vehicles. A movie crew.

He holds the girl in his thin trembling arms. "This is better."

It's still raining. It rained all night. In the morning, there had been a break, accompanied by a scurry of activity. A man in an enormous yellow raincoat, looking like a big duck, stomped around in puddles, a line of ducklings scurrying after him with their clipboards and their viewfinders. A door opened on a truck revealing a dozen ape-suits. A handsome face appeared in the window of a trailer. Then the rain pounded again and everyone disappeared.

He's shaking. The baby has his sweater and his coat and most of the sheets from the clean bin of the laundry truck. But the rain is coming down so hard that he can wash some diapers by simply holding them out the window. He counts that as a miracle. The smell is almost too much.

It's strange, all this luck. He was crazy to take the baby, crazy to steal this truck. He was thinking crazy when he drove into the woods – he just wanted to get away from the police.

But he was lucky to find this camp. Lucky to have a place to hide. All kinds of luck piling up. Or are they miracles?

Either way, he's not in control.

A crack on the glass. "Some storm" quacks the baby duck, passing in a bag. "I'll be back at dinnertime." He opens the bag and unwraps the contents. A sandwich. An apple.

A bottle of milk. Another miracle.

The baby is crying. The whole crew is staring.

Cameras are rolling, so he's safe for now. Clay picks up the pace, skirting the circle of apes. They wave their arms above their heads, threatening the fur-clad gal. Mocking her.

She screams and the baby's wails rise in pitch.

Clay steadies the makeshift backpack that holds his child and heads up a steep hill. The woods are thick above. If he can reach them before the director stops the action, he's sure he can flee undisturbed. He's seen enough of this operation to know that these fellahs are working on the cheap. They won't interrupt a decent shot just to stop a stranger fleeing with a baby.

His legs pump and he wants to scream.

He crashes into the woods.

"And…cut!"

Clay wakes in the cave and tries to remember his dream. He'd been on a sailboat with his brother. Richard had slipped and grabbed his arm.

The baby stirs beside him. He wraps the blanket tighter, shielding her from the wind blowing in from the cave's mouth. The blanket had just appeared one morning. As did the food and the milk. Someone left these things outside. He guesses it was the film crew.

They're all gone now. How long? He doesn't know that. What does he know? That he's sick.

That he's dying?

Yes, Richard had slipped but somehow it was him that ended up in the water. Somehow it was Clay. He sank and he sank. But he didn't drown.

Instead, he saw a whole city down there. A city of beautiful new buildings and streets made entirely of little specks of gold. An architectural wonder. But in the windows and on the boulevard were dead men. Sitting behind desks and riding in cars – all of them corpses.

He's sick all right, but somehow he thinks that taking the baby was Richard's idea.

He hears voices now.

"Shall we kill this man?"

"Let us kill the *baby*."

Is this part of his dream? Or are there men outside the cave? Dirty men. Hobos. Can they see him? Is this real?

It is. The pain as they beat him makes that clear.

They leave with the baby. They leave him alone to despair and to die.

Despite the beatings, Clay can still see through one eye. He stares at the hobos by the fire. It took everything he had to drag himself here. And now he's going to die. Under a dead tree. In a pile of dead branches. A few feet from the only thing he ever wanted.

Richard told him to take the baby and run. Richard said that Dora was sick with grief over the other twin. He said that she would kill the girl. He said that Clay had to act quickly. He said Clay had to act now.

He feels a chill on his neck which surprises him. He thought he'd lost all feeling back there.

What if his brother was lying?

"I'm not for hurting her, Jeb. She might be worth some money."

"What I have in mind won't hurt much. Give her here."

The old man doesn't want to see it. He turns away

from the fire, and right into the hard end of a swinging branch. It rips his face off.

Clay lumbers from the brush, top-heavy, his head swollen. The bigger hobo drops the baby and grabs a flaming log. He breaks Clay's arm. He breaks Clay's shoulder.

Clay lunges and they both end up in the fire. Clay feels the flames on his hands, on his legs. They both scream. They both burn.

The hobo panics first, a ball of flame bobbing through the dark woods.

Clay rolls from the fire. And there she is.

His daughter.

Lightning flashes, illuminating cages. The animals thrash wildly. The air smells of wet fur and mange.

Clay carries his tiny bundle down the muddy hill and through the zoo. He's sobbing and moaning but the baby is quiet.

He can see the lights of Los Angeles down the canyon. He and the baby begin the long trek, leaving behind Griffith Park and their home of two weeks.

One of her girls left the shed door open again. Minnie runs from the house through the pouring rain and there she finds the monster.

He beckons in his filthy rags. He twists his broken frame and points. His mouth contorts and he moans and he points.

"…she's no orphan…she has a mother…a father… she needs more than I can give her…needs to stay here…"

He's pointing at the sign mounted near the roof. **Minnie Barton Home for Girls.**

"…Richard said my wife would kill the baby…that's why I took her, why we hid away…am I a villain? … am I a fool? …a patsy?"

She steps inside the shed. She's glad he keeps talking. It gives her time to open the locked box she keeps there.

"I am not those things. I am her father. I am her dad!"

He's raising the baby in his arms when she shoots him.

"Shame!" she cries. "Shame on you! Shame! Shame!"

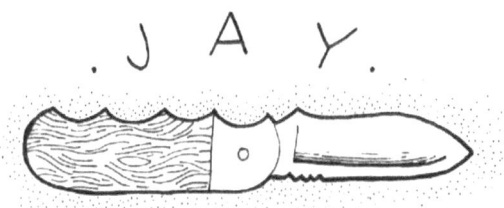

1970

It's a one-lane road heading deep into the middle of nowhere and we're stuck behind the school bus with the psychedelic paint-job. The fucking peace symbol on the back door is bouncing in my face – it's been doing that for hours. It looks like a chicken-foot. It looks like the foot on a cartoon chicken. This is the symbol of my generation?

"Breathe."

This way of life has run its course, its bedrock philosophy proven bankrupt, and the group of followers have grown smaller and smaller, scattered in the wilderness, ceaselessly chasing their lost summer. And we trail along behind them.

"Breathe, daddy."

These ideas of mine aren't even fresh. I've seen plenty of peace symbols, and had plenty of time to ruminate on them, over the last…what? Three years? Shit, since Josey was seven. What a waste.

"C'mon, daddy. Breathe." She strokes my arm. My little girl, keeping me sane.

Our caravan finally reaches the river. The psychedelic bus coughs out hippies and the rest of the clan gathers to welcome us. It's a blur of free expression. Jesters prance and play. Dirty cherubs tumble in the grass.

I park the van and Josey starts setting up. A couple of clowns take a break from hanging banners in the trees to check out our wares. I eyeball their finger-painting: '*Make Love!*' '*Love is All!*' '*All You Need is LOVE!*'

"I *love* your beard," says the groovy gal, offering a joint. I don't take it and I don't love my beard. She bats her lashes.

Groovy guy bristles, "You holding, *dad*?" I shake my head. He lifts his tinted shades, his sclera red and grey. "You should see things though my eyes, man. It would blow your mind."

Josey bows her head and cups her hands, saying a silent prayer. I know she's praying for restraint.

Sorry, baby. I'm going to kill this guy. Tonight.

The loons are laughing it up. They've got an old projector running off a car battery, throwing a black and white flick at a sheet hung up in the trees. It's "Tarzan" and the heroine is drowning in a flickering mass of crazy apes.

And here comes the hoots. "Give it up for the monkey man, baby!" and "Animal love forever!" and, somehow, "Have a nice day, LBJ!"

It doesn't matter what you say, funny or not, this crowd is high and everything gets a laugh. The triumph of equality, I guess.

I've been waiting for a long time, but even groovy guys have gotta shit sooner or later. This one finally makes his move to the woods. I follow. I have the photo of my wife in my hand and it trembles. Once I show it to him, he has to die.

His reactions follow a familiar pattern — the jokes, the lame protestations, a pathetic attempt at bravado.

The sharp cry of pain when I break his arm is nothing new. But he surprises me with his expression when he sees the knife – he knows he's going to die.

So I show him the photo.

The second surprise. "I seen her! Saratoga, man, I seen her with Mackey. They call him Doctor Mackey. The Magic Man. In Saratoga!"

My grip loosens on his throat. This is unprecedented. The guy is cooperating and he has some real information. A sudden flood of doubt about the sanctity of my mission. Questions of ethics, they crowd my mind…

He shakes loose and gets one, two, three steps before my resolve returns.

Josey.

I drop him and I go to work with the knife. It isn't pretty, and it isn't easy, but I keep in mind that this guy willfully shrugged off any meaningful masculinity years ago.

I'm just making it manifest.

"Which one's your favorite?"

"My favorite what, sweetie?"

"Your favorite gas station, of course."

"The Shell station in Wichita."

"Why?"

"You remember the guy who tried to sell me the transistor radio?"

"Yeah."

"His teeth were the color of your hair."

"Oh daddy, you say the nicest things."

"Your turn, Josey."

"Your favorite car we've seen today."

"Just one?"

"That's the rules, daddy."

"Then the tan Rambler we passed at Lake Tahoe. No, it was the orange VW van."

"That's two, daddy."

"Which is your favorite?"

"The orange one. But I'm lying."

"The truth then! Out with it!"

"This one, daddy, cuz I'm here with you."

1883

She's ten now and she finally has a name. For a long time it was Cutie, followed by Girlie and then, one day, she was Sunday.

They've been riding for a long time and the desert doesn't change. She couldn't guess how her father knows when to stop, but he does. He lifts her from her horse.

"Do you remember this place?"

She doesn't so she wanders here and there. She kicks scrub. She gets on her knees and plays with the coarse sand.

Her father is back in the saddle, scanning the horizon. She brushes the hair from her face and watches. His eyes are swallowed by the shadow of his hat. Grey hairs sprinkle across the black field of his mustache. He's moving a little slower these days. But he's still the strongest man she has ever seen.

Something sparkles in the sand. It's a tarnished silver necklace. She hangs it around her neck. She digs around a little and finds some more jewelry. And then some childrens' toys — a sling-shot, a couple of ragged dolls.

And bones. Lots and lots of bones.

. C L A Y .

1923

There is a mob outside the temple. Believers outnumber the one hundred wary police by fifty to one. They keep coming, piling from autos, leaping from trolley cars.

Jubilant!

A fresh division of uniformed cops forms a phalanx and busts the crowd in two at Sunset Boulevard. They usher through a flat-bed truck. It's a float, a miniature version of the Angelus Temple itself. A banner hangs from the carnation cross atop the rose-covered dome, **"Announcing The Opening Of The Church Of The Foursquare Gospel."**

As the float passes through the crowd, a murmur travels with it. "It has come straight from the Tournament of Roses." "It's won the Grand Marshal's prize." "God bless Sister and her work."

Following behind the float, swept through the crowd in its wake, limps a hideous figure clutching a small bundle.

Deacons move among the faithful, ushering the crippled and the lame to the aisles. The news spreads through the auditorium and into the balconies; Sister will be doing no healings on this day, the first day of the new Temple.

Lights dim and the ceiling glows. All, converted and curious alike, lift their eyes to see painted clouds cross the baby-blue sky. The choir begins to sing. Their voices soar; they crescendo!

Sister Aimee Semple McPherson appears on the altar. Her white robes shimmer in a hot blaze of spotlight. A bouquet of roses burns bright red in her hands. "How do you like the new Gospel tent?" Cheers erupt from the gathered multitude. "Its sloping poles are now pillars, its sagging roof a mighty dome.

The openings that showed the evening stars have now become arched windows, and through them stream the light of His blessing…"

Everyone is caught up in her words, the new temple, the uplifting notes of the orchestra, the choir.

No one sees the cripple until he's nearly at the altar.

His head is enormous, swollen and matted with blood. One arm hangs useless beneath a bulging shoulder. He drags himself forward on stiff legs. His ragged clothing smells of smoke. A trail of blood stains the carpet beneath his bare and mud-caked feet.

Sister halts her sermon mid-sentence. Ushers rush forward but she stops them with her upheld hands. The choir's hymn is swallowed whole by the sudden silence.

The man is lifting a pile of rags towards her. She kneels and takes the filthy bundle. Inside is a tiny baby girl.

Her eyes connect with Clay.

Just before he collapses, a moment of true and magnificent love passes between them.

A pile of flesh and bandages lies on a stone floor. Ragged breath. Clay is alive but just.

He wakes to find a note. "Go to the yard. Climb to freedom. All is taken care of." It is signed, "A friend."

He gives the cell door a tentative tug. It opens freely. He stumbles down a dark passage, past cages where other broken men are dying.

There's the rope. He struggles to the top of the prison wall.

The city spreads before him like a grey blanket littered with light. Beyond is the darkness. He knows what's out there. He knows Griffith Park is out there.

He wraps the rope around and around his neck and he leaps.

. J A Y .

1970

Josey is jumping rope with some kids outside the Saratoga Market. The place is packed with hippies, goofing on the locals and loading up on supplies.

It's going to rain soon. I close the door to the phonebooth.

"So what happens if Phoebe's there? What do you do then?"

"I don't know." I've been looking for her for three years, and I still don't know.

"I'm going to be candid, Jay. We've been friends for a long time but a lot has changed since we last talked. I quit the University and became a cop. Brooklyn Academy. A year on the beat. A few more in a squad car. I just got my star. Call it penance, call it what you will."

I start to say something about crossing to the other

side but I stop. When did I stop believing in sides? When did I ever believe in them?

A mini-bus scoots past. I scan the windows. Evan continues. "What I do all day is ask difficult questions. So let me ask you a few. What do you expect to happen when you find Phoebe? That she'll be well again? That she'll want to be with her daughter? That she'll want to be with you? Do you want to hold her? Do you want to hit her? What?"

I can't say "save her" so I don't say anything.

Some jokesters are performing impromptu street theater. They parade around with a battered trunk. A bearded fool puts on a police hat and goose-steps. Girls in face-paint kneel in worship before a runt dressed as an A-bomb.

"One thing is for sure. If you find her, then you gotta ask Josey what she wants. You gotta do that."

I hang up, imagining that conversation. Suddenly, I hope I never find my wife. The sky opens up and drenches the street, washing the filth from the hippies' caravan.

And that's when I see her with the Magic Man.

I lead Josey to the middle of the field. The Gathering is calling it "Enlightenment Meadow." She gives me a look. We strictly avoid these places.

"Grab a knee." She laughs. It's our little joke, transforming the ever-present hand-holding circle of love into a football huddle.

I can't remember what I've told her and what I've left out. So I tell her everything.

I tell her about meeting her mother. About our life at the University, our little house, Phoebe's studies, my teaching position. I tell her about dropping out. About the work commune in Alaska. About her birth.

"Was it me that made her run away?"

"No, Josey."

"Was it me that turned her crazy?"

The madness was always there, waiting to take her. "It was my fault. We left our old life because of my problems with my father, my problems with my life. Your mother was safer in our old world. There was structure there. There were steady friends, her family."

I try to push away the city of tents. Someone's on a makeshift stage, playing a guitar and singing, *"Why don't we swing along the road…"*

"This transient world, this traveling circus, it's no good. It feeds her sickness."

"Is that why sometimes you get angry at these people?"

"Yes," I say. I don't say, 'that's why sometimes I kill these people.'

A bearded troll is shouting from the stage. "I hear the call! I hear the call and I will answer it!" The crowd comes running on their bare dirty feet. The Magic Man is about to speak.

"We can turn around right now, Josey. I mean it."

"No. I want to meet my mother."

THE OLD MAN.

1970

An army-surplus tent has been mounted to the bed of the truck, making it a modern covered wagon. The old man has a good view from inside. He can see both the crowd and the speaker.

The Magic Man shouts. He prances. He spreads his arms and they encompass the Gathering. "Consider the vortex, friends, the black hole. It's out there. It's just over that hill. It lives in the cities and it eats tall buildings. You can read it in the papers, man, in the black and in the white. The vortex is the Makers' work. The Makers are hungry. They're tired of the skyscrapers.

They're coming for you. They're coming for me!"

A photograph of a young man jitters in the old man's hands. He reports. *"That's Mackey out there, son. I think his name is John. They call him 'The Magic Man'. He's a curly mane on a matchstick. He used to be on TV. He was the lead guy in that TV version of "Jessup", the film about the hippy cop. I seen him a couple of times now. At San Luis Obispo in '68, up in Boulder that same year, and twice in Saratoga both in '69 and now."*

Mackey drops to his knees, draping an American flag over his head as a shawl. "They say our movement is dying! I say that it's them that's dying! *La morte*, motherfuckers! *Adiós!*" And here's a Nazi salute.

"He considers himself a ladies man and he probably is. There's a bunch of gals around him generally. I've seen him with a girl named Sara Blue, used to come around here with her hand-made whistles. Jewel Something, Missy Something. Lately, it's a pretty gal named Phoebe. Phoebe James has sad eyes. She told me she missed her little girl."

He's back on his feet! "If you're feeling sick, don't fear. The Magic Man has Magic Hands. If you feel the Makers holding you down, pulling you down, just reach out. The Magic Man has Magic hands."

The photo could be of the old man's son. Or maybe

it's just him as a young man. "*Sounds like he can heal the sick and raise the dead. This is getting mighty familiar, my dear boy.*"

Mackey's speeches nearly always arouse the libido; couples begin to drift off into the surrounding woods.

One unfortunate pair makes the discovery, stumbling upon the corpse of Josey's mother, her throat slit and looking as pale as a paper doll.

1888

Sunday stares up at the damned thing, considering all the threads in the rope of a noose. There are far too many to count.

It's much easier to do the math on the folk who died hanging from those gallows.

Twenty-four were men from Los Rios — they were Arango's men and her father's personal enemies.

Thirty-one were his old friends.

The remaining seven were made up of local cow thieves, bad drunks and one drifter from Ohio who had the misfortune of being named Jesse James.

Sixty-two.

Waring is dying. This morning, she had the deputies haul his bed out in to the sunlight. Now the sun is dipping low and the gallows' shadow has nearly consumed him.

He starts and grips her hands. His eyes struggle to focus. He fills his lungs one last time and breathes out, "I am your father."

In fifteen years, she had never questioned it.

Now she knew he was lying.

She considered burning a lot of things.

The chapel where he knelt and prayed and didn't believe. The birthing tent where he played God to screaming women and newborns. The hammock where he spent his evenings. The house where she slept, dreaming that she was his daughter.

In the end, Sunday put a torch to the saloon he never entered. And the gallows, the goddamn gallows where he strung up each of his friends and most of his enemies.

Then she turned her back on the flames and left town at a gallop. Headed south to Mexico. To find her real father.

The latest of herd of cattle has arrived in Dodge City, and with it plenty of hands with money in them. The muddy streets are transformed to a world of amusements, all for a coin. Or several coins. Or every coin.

Benton blames that damn carnival for giving him the image. Without it, his dreams could just go on being mean and angry without taking any specific form.

But now, every night, there is a shooting gallery. Targets rattle along, each the head of someone he knows. He shoots and they pitch backwards.

Ka-DING! Ka-DING! Ka-DING!

All through the night.

Maybe if he heads south, down towards Arizona, maybe Mexico...

Sunday rides into the last town before the border. She spends most of what's left of Waring's money on a fresh mount. Now she only needs to find someone to trust. Where she's going, it's not a good idea to be a woman riding alone. It's late so every suitable candidate is in the saloon.

She spots him right away.

A murderous bunch of cowhands are converging on a drunken and unlucky farmer. He's backing up the stairs, ranting through his fear. He's outnumbered and about to get clobbered.

There's a whistle. The big guy at the bar tosses him a stool. The farmer catches it and goes to town. He gets clobbered anyway, but, as these things go, he had a better shot with the stool.

Benton provides another stool for Sunday. He smiles like an old friend. Sunday quickly realizes that Benton is smarter than his size would suggest. She watches his eyes as he listens, taking her words in, considering them.

He'll do.

Inside his head, he only hears one thing. *Ka-DING!*

Benton suffers from mental illness. He tries to cover it with alcohol, but Sunday can smell the madness beneath the whiskey.

His rants fill their tent. He brays. He prays. He elaborates on the matter that consumes him. The Pressure he feels. The Eyes that watch him. The Pressure to be good. The Eyes that judge him.

This time he tries to hurt her. She's ready, bashing his head with a pot then turning her father's gun on him. Benton is bleeding as he stumbles into the night, still braying, still praying.

She gathers her stuff. It's time to leave town.

A thought stops her.

The preacher halts mid-sermon. The congregation can hear it too. Someone is shouting outside the gospel tent, bellowing like an injured animal.

With a sudden WHOOSH, the tent behind the preacher is streaked with fire. Worshippers scramble and scream. The altar erupts in flames. The preacher is trapped. He's doomed.

But through the fiery wall rides Sunday Waring, bareback on a charging stallion. She grabs the preacher at full gallop and lifts him into the saddle.

"Hold tight, Padre!" Sunday gives her mount the spurs and horse and riders leap over believers.

Benton's bellowing from outside takes form "Shut his Eyes! Shut his Eyes!" as a burning hay wagon hits the tent and explodes in an enormous fireball.

"Do you miss your flock?"

He turns pages on his bible as he rides. "My flock is who I am with."

"And what about your faith?"

"I carry it here."

"And if you lose your black book?"

"I carry it in here too." He touches his heart.

"You're a lucky man, Padre."

When she reckons that she is just a hard day's ride away from Los Rios, Sunday ditches the preacher. His name is David and he has been a good traveling companion. He's not too handy with a gun or anything else, but he does make for an imposing figure on his dark horse, tall and slender, dressed head to toe in Man of God black.

When she asked him to join up with her, Sunday figured that riding with anybody was better than riding alone. Over the last hundred some miles, she'd been proved right a number of times.

But he's too damn good for what she has in mind. So she slips off into the night and points her mount deeper into Mexico, towards the town her father founded and named.

She rides with the reins in her mouth. Hissing his name. "Arango."

Sunday dismounts onto the deserted streets of Los Rios. A door on an adobe hangs off its hinges. She pushes it open, revealing a room that tells a story – a crib where a *madre* lay her *niña* – both left to die in the desert by the man who called himself her father. There's a bed where an *hombre* once slept, an *hombre* who later traveled north and got hung up on the gallows by that same man.

The identical story is repeated all down the street. Los Rios is a ghost town.

And Arango is a ghost. He sits outside his sun-bleached hacienda with the caved-in roof, looking just as collapsed and drained of color.

He unfolds himself and stands. He shrugs and beckons the girl inside. As he leads her to a chair and brings her a warm glass of milk, he passes a mirror and catches his reflection for the first time in…how long? A long time.

So his first question surprises her. "When did I get so old?"

The stove smokes. A long time has passed since it has been lit. Sunday and Arango sit cross-legged on a hand-woven rug with a diamond pattern. The old man pours beads of many colors and sizes from a leather bag. They land in a formless pile between them.

Arango picks out a blue bead and threads it onto a long piece of string. He passes it to his daughter. Sunday threads a silver one and passes it back. The string moves silently between them in this way until Arango asks, "Shall I tell you the story of how Coyote tricked the wind?"

Sunday nods.

"Coyote was wandering in the desert and he came to a great lake. Coyote was lazy and did not want to travel so far around the lake, so he said to the Water, 'Water, why don't you move aside so that I can cross here?' Well, Water was lazy too, so she said, 'No, no. You must walk around, Coyote.' Coyote looked at the long trail around the lake and said, 'You must move to one side or maybe to the other and I will walk across.' But still, Water would not move. So Coyote called to his friend the Wind and he whispered in his ear. 'Do you hear what Water says? She brags that she is stronger than you. She tells the world that you cannot make her move.' Wind was angry and he blew and he blew at the water. But Water would not move so Wind blew some more. And as he blew, the air grew very hot and soon the Water boiled and soon it disappears completely. Coyote was very happy and he crosses the lake. But half-way across, he got very, very thirsty and there was no water. This is how we got the Santa Ana winds, which still blow hot when the Wind is angry. And this is how Coyote came to die of thirst at the bottom of a lake."

Sunday starts. The pile of beads is gone and between Arango's nimble fingers shines a finished necklace.

He gently places it around her neck.

Arango opens the door to the baby's room. A thin layer of sand covers the floor. It covers the crib. A mural grows from the nearest wall like a vine, stretching into the dark room.

"Your mother," Arango whispers. "Before you were born."

Sunday's candle follows the narrative — a woman in the window of a log cabin — a handsome man in a silver-studded saddle — a dark shadow with a black hat and scarf — lovers entwined — the shadow shrinking before a glowing sunburst — a map of the trail south — the smiling man and woman holding hands, the glow now coming from the woman's belly…

The chalk paintings abruptly halt. Sunday knows why. She imagines the pictures. The woman dead — the crib empty — the shadow escaping with the baby into the desert.

Arango quietly weeps. Sunday takes his hand. She gives him some chalk.

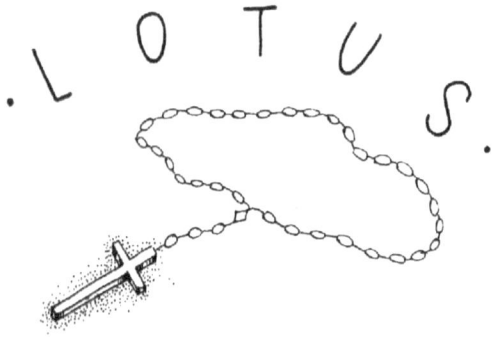

LOTUS

1947

Dora

Her given name is Dora but everyone in her circle knows her as Lady Richard. If Richard Lawrence isn't the King of Los Angeles, he's definitely royalty. He's grabbed a handful of every land-grab since Owens Valley. His Boar Enterprises owns a hefty chunk of Hollywood real estate and built a good quarter of the buildings downtown.

With royalty comes obligation and so Lady does her part as a member in good standing of the Soroptimists, the woman's branch of the Optimists Club. Today's obligation involves attendance at the dedication of some benches circled by cement and rocks in a wooded area of Griffith Park.

The president of the Soroptimists speaks to the gathered crowd. She's a mountain of a woman with a habit of emphasizing many words. "We dedicate this *haven* of solitude and comfort in memory of *Minnie Barton*, a woman who offered *respite* to many when they needed it most. As the *second* female policewoman in Los Angeles, Miss Barton founded her *Home for Girls* in *1917*, housing young women on parole or discharged from *prison*."

Dora should be listening but instead her mind is filled with the strangest vision. She imagines Mary sleeping close to Joseph, an empty manger beside them; Mary's eyes suddenly open, she knows the baby is coming.

Lotus

Lotus has been staring at the bouquet in her hands since the ceremony began. It is designed to represent Chastity and Recovered Innocence and is meant to be identical to the others girls', though Lotus has discovered that hers has one more lily than the girl to her right, and one less daisy than the girl on her left.

"Ten years later, Minnie Barton founded the *Bide-A-*

Wee Home for destitute woman with *small* children. We recognize the delegation here today from the organization she founded before her death, *The Big Sister League*. We also thank the representatives from *the Foursquare Gospel Church,* especially the young ladies who were taken in as *orphans* by Aimee Semple McPherson and raised by her church."

The crowd musters some light applause for Lotus and the dozen other young and discarded women who live at the Temple. Sister Aimee gave her the name Lotus after returning from a missionary trip to China where she discovered that lovely and delicate flower.

"We will now begin the *formal* dedication. Welcome Richard Lawrence's *wife*, Dora, to do the honor of *cutting* the ribbon."

Lotus is unaware that twenty-three years ago, not far from where she stands, her father held her in his arms while the woman they are honoring shot him in the chest.

She is also unaware that the imposing lady approaching with the scissors is her mother. The woman's eyes find hers and they fill with a sudden look of shock and recognition. She straightens and collapses in a dead faint.

Lotus drops her bouquet and, somehow, catches Dora's limp and falling form. She gently lays her on the hard ground, scattered lilies and daisies surrounding her head.

Richard

Richard Lawrence is a man with a firm grasp on the world and where he fits in it. He is a man with ideas. One day he plans to make a film which will elucidate those ideas and educate the people who see it.

If this were that film, and he were a character in it, he would look directly into the camera and say this to the audience:

"I am The Builder. I look at a landscape dotted with scattered and randomly placed communities and I see a City Of The Future.

"This is how it works. It starts with a vision. Then I plan it. And then I build it.

"We took the water we needed from the Owens Valley and brought it to Los Angeles. My colleagues and I transformed a cow town into a city. And then we saw a filthy slum, an opium den, a Chinatown. I had a vision of a clean replica, a safe facsimile which tourists would travel to see, to shop and to spend money. And then I planned it. And then I built *two* of them, and I called them New Chinatown and China City. I filled both with happy yellow people dressed in native garb selling exotic food and wares. And in the place of that old slum, I built a train station, which I named Union Station, to bring more of those tourists to my city. To bring them faster and fatter and full of money.

"We have a newspaper in our City Of The Future which reports only good news. No murders or crimes or civil unrest happen here. Nothing to frighten the people away. The weather report is always on the front page and the weather is always good.

"I stand outside history. History is on the wrong track. The wrong people won the last two world wars. I am The Builder. I build things."

The Lawrences drove their brand new Lincoln Zephyr straight from the storefront window in Hollywood to Palm Springs, with only a quick stop in Bel Air to load their bags and pick up Richard's nurse.

The car now sits just outside the desert town. It's

covered in dust and muck. Richard, who insisted on driving, lies on the hard ground. His breathing is even more labored that usual.

Dora holds an umbrella, shielding Richard's sallow face from the brutal sun. An urgent whisper to the nurse. "Get help. Find a doctor. Hurry."

Lotus does hurry. She pulls up her long skirt and sprints across the hot sand towards town. She is not content to let the old man die out here.

She wants to kill him herself.

She's alone with Richard. She can hear the doctor talking to Dora outside the door. He's telling her that they can't move Richard, that he has serious respiratory problems. He'll have to stay in this little hut in the desert until he gets better or stops breathing.

She has a pillow. It's going to be easy to kill him. And justified. She knows who she is now.

Over the last year, she's pieced together the whole story. She was born to Dora and Clay Lawrence in 1923, one of a pair of twins. Her sister died a few days later. Dora was distraught, sick with grief. Clay thought Dora would kill the other baby, that she would kill Lotus. Clay fled with the baby. Over the next two weeks, he was beaten, burnt, and shot. He hung himself in prison.

How did these tragic events come to be? Richard arranged them. He wanted Dora for himself, a queen for his growing empire. But he didn't want a daughter. He'd known how to manipulate his brother since they were little boys. Clay had been born with as weak a grasp on reality as Richard's was strong.

Richard simply set him in motion.

Now it is twenty-four years later and she works for Richard. Dora has a new name now. Everyone calls her "Lady". Lady knows Lotus is her daughter but continues to pretend she's just a nurse. Richard doesn't suspect a thing.

She finds a photo in Richard's wallet. She's never seen her father. The photo is old, but there is something else. She rubs the crusty substance on its surface. It's spit. It has been spit upon over and over for many years. Dried, flaked and spit upon again.

Such hate. But somehow she has survived. Somehow she is in this room. There must be a purpose and the purpose is clear. To kill this monster. For her father, for herself, for any one who might be destroyed by

Richard in the future.

She places the pillow over his face.

She curses God. She curses the church that took her in. The church that saved her life.

If only he were awake. If only he were praying for his eternal soul. Then she could do it.

She turns away.

. J A Y .

1970

The booth is ridiculously close to the highway. I grab the phone almost before it rings.

"You heard right, Jay. It was Phoebe. I talked with the Saratoga police, told them that my Captain had me on a similar case here in New York, that I was following up on a similar MO. Lacerations on her face and hands… It's ugly… You want to hear this?"

"I want it all, Evan."

"Death was either by strangulation or blood loss. She had bruise marks on her neck, but then again, her throat was slit… All of it?"

"All of it."

"Recent sexual activity. Possibly rape."

"It's all bad."

"Not everything. The state police took over the case.

They are taking an interest in this, Jay. Dead hippies are piling up all over the state. As much as they'd like to ignore Phoebe's murder, they can't. At least, not yet."

"What do you mean?"

"They'll keep looking for her killer for as long as they don't have a suspect. But given a way out, like, say, an abandoned husband who was in the vicinity of the murder…they'd drop the investigation in two seconds flat."

I press my head against the glass.

"What do I do?"

"You want that answer from a friend or a police officer?"

"Both."

"They don't know about you. Keep it that way. Disappear. Don't show your face until they catch the killer. You know a place?"

"Yes, I do." A truck clatters past, in low gear because of the grade. On the other side of the highway squats a roadside bar and, next to it, a sign reading "Welcome to Silverlode, Colorado."

I cross the highway and begin the next chapter in my life with my father.

The high-altitude glare off the highway is so bright that Josey and I are mostly blind when we step into the dark bar. She holds my hand tight.

Tired cowboys drink bottled beer. Their necks are bent and the brims of their hats nearly touch the bar. Only the bartender looks up.

"I'm looking for directions. Up to the Lucas place."

"Why you want to go up there?"

"I'm his son."

A stool scrapes and I get a real close look at a face. It's red and getting redder. I watch the cowboy's hands. Clenching. Clenching.

My own hands move and Josey is behind me.

"Going out for some air." He stomps into the light. More scraping. The rest follow him out.

Now it's just Josey and me and the bartender. He picks up a phone and dials.

Josey

There's a terrible argument going on in the parking lot. Josey watches from a distance.

"Lucas' instructions are precise. Clients are not allowed to have their vehicles on the property," says the tall young one.

"We are not *'clients!'*" Josey's never seen her dad so angry. It's a sight. But her eyes keep wandering up to the mountains. It's amazing how an imperceptible change of light down here signals an operatic drama of shifting shadow on the towering peaks.

A defeated shout! Jay hands the VW's keys to the old guy who calls himself Critter. The tall young one is called Mr. Marks, and he just keeps saying "it is necessary, it is necessary" over and over.

She follows their van as Critter backs it into a large cinder-block structure. Parked inside are dozens of expensive looking cars. She recognizes BMWs and Mercedes. Critter rattles shut a heavy metal gate and locks it.

She asks Critter, "Fight over?"

He spits in his hands. "Yep."

She sits next to Mr. Marks in the back. He's trying to explain.

"This is extremely atypical. Both of our vans are currently transporting clients to the airport."

They're all jammed in Critter's old truck, bouncing over a mountain road, flanked by thick forest. The radio plays loud static. Her dad is annoyed. "Why don't you turn that shit off?"

"Can't." Critter brushes at dirty hair with dirty fingers. "It's wired t' on."

"You ever get reception?"

"Only when I'm too far from home."

The truck stops. A cowboy greeting: the branded wood banner swings softly above an electric fence.

"The Ranch"
A Place for Positive Change

Lucas

Lucas James pauses to scan this audience. He's spoken to packed stadiums but the net worth of the people in this room exceeds the tens of thousands there. Of the Fortune 500, he's looking at a good fifth of them. Their wardrobes are a near perfect blend of rustic and expensive, much like the lodge in which they sit. Most of them have his book in their laps. And he's got them in the palm of his hand.

"After ten days of study, of *work*, we prepare to return, transformed, to the world. It's a world full of changing attitudes towards love, towards sexuality, towards monogamy, towards traditional family structures. It's a freer world. Are *we* to be denied these freedoms because of our *standing*? Our *success*? Our *wealth*? These will no longer be barriers to us. We have learned the power of Self-Actualizing Narrative. Using the Four Life Principles, we now know that every life is a story and that how we tell that story is up to us! Does the story of Icarus have to be about a man who flew too close to the sun? Or can it be about a man who dreamed the impossible, achieved the impossible, and gladly gave his life to do so."

He lifts the book. "My Story, Your Story."

"Let's look again at my life. My story. Age 24, full professor at Yale. Head of my department before I was 30. Awards, money, recognition as a man of knowledge and accomplishment. Life was going great. I was coasting. Content. And then my wife, my beloved Marie, became sick. And for all my money, and my titles, and my stature in my field, I couldn't do a damn thing. I was trapped by societal expectations, I was emasculated, forced to play the prescribed roles. The loyal husband. The selfless father. The grieving widow. And then, one day, I realized what I had to do. I had to…"

The group speaks as one, "Get Over Myself!"

"Principle four."

"Denying Joy is Denying Life."

"Number three."

"The Past is a Prison."

"I retook possession of myself. I took a close look and I saw myself anew. I understood myself not as a man who had lost his wife, but as a man who had survived his grief. You've all faced loss this week! Learned humility in the face of pain!"

"And climbed back out!"

"*Dug* your way out, tooth and nail, back to the light! You've done this! You've read my book. You've adopted my principles. You have completed the program. You are over yourselves."

Lucas summons something close to Grace.

"Now go and enjoy your wealth!"

Jay

Dad finishes his little speech and his followers jump up, full of chatter. They love the guy.

I watch Josey staring. She is seeing her grandfather for the first time. I wonder what he looks like to her. I try to look with fresh eyes, but I see the same thing. A man so used to intimidating people that he long ago stopped trying.

The great man raises his hand and everyone gets quiet.

"There is one more story I want to share with you. It's an old story, perhaps a familiar one. About a father who lost his son. A son who traveled to foreign lands and became lost."

Across the room, his piercing eyes lock on mine.

"This is a story I've never told, because until now it didn't have an ending. But now it does. The prodigal son has returned. My own son, Lucas James Junior!"

A spotlight swings our way and the entire room turns as one to look at us. Josey blinks in the harsh light.

The old man and the kid

As he always does, the old man sits beneath the tent mounted on the back of his flat-bed truck. But he's not alone. He's been talking for two days straight and his visitor has never looked tired. In fact, the young guy leans toward him, hungry for more words.

The old man pulls two sketches from a journal on a shelf crowded with journals. "These two are the last I seen with your sister." He arranges them among the dozen other sketches that cover the metal flooring. "This here is Jay James. And this is his daughter, Josey. She's near twelve, I would believe."

The kid nods and nods and prods. "More."

The old man never thought he'd grow tired of sharing this information. The honest fact is that he has been waiting for a long time for someone just like this eager and motivated fellow. He's been waiting for him to come along and take what he had gathered and do *something* with it. Do *anything* with it.

But, now that he's here, the old man finds it tiring. Yet the words keep coming.

"Jay James is an interesting guy. Ex-professor at Stanford, dropped out, dropped WAY the hell out, ended up on a work commune up in Alaska. Baby

Josey comes along, his wife loses her mind, splits on them both. She starts making the scene, she's traveling the circuit, looking for a new life, and he's following right behind her, looking for her. He and the daughter got an orange VW bus and they sell a bunch of stuff from it at the Gatherings –- leather goods, pipes and such, other sundries — pays for the journey."

"He ever find his wife?"

"I don't know. She turned up in a field not far from here. Dead like your sister."

The young man picks up Jay's sketch, it shakes in his hands. "Where is he?"

"I don't know that either. Though you may have heard of his dad. Lucas."

"Lucas **James**?!"

"That's him."

"*Everybody's* heard of Lucas James!"

Lucas closes the door to his private study. When 'the great man' is angry, his language climbs right over the top, getting damn near Shakespearean. "What atrocity must I have committed in a past life? Did I routinely kick cripples down stone stairs? Did I take a torch to a crowded cathedral?"

"My exploits aren't nearly as notorious as you want to believe."

"It's your very nature that is my curse. The terrible fact is this — within you dwell two elements which should be at war but instead are *married*: your intelligence and your attraction to the lowest of mankind. It is this twisted nature which led you to throw away your education, your life, everything, for these *pigs*! And further horrors — you *continue* to lie with these pigs, to wallow in their filth, to drag your daughter to their festivals and their gatherings, their full retreats from civilization."

I'm completely honest with him. "When I joined the commune, I committed to living by some good ideas. They're still good ideas. But they got twisted together with some very bad ideas by some very weak people. I knew all this years ago. I wanted to leave, to start over somewhere with my wife and my daughter. But Phoebe wouldn't leave that life. She was ill, she was confused, she ran away. So, I followed. I searched for her for three years.

"For *three years*, I followed her trail through the decaying movement. For *three years*, the failure of those good ideas was in my face, a constant reminder of my mistake and the mistake of history. These laughing, prancing fools, celebrating the failure of their revolution, underlining every rotten turn they took. It did horrible things to me. And I, in turn, did horrible things to them.

"So hold your tongue, old man, these years have been punishment enough."

My father surprises me by wrapping me in a bear hug. I don't know what he means by it. But I want to be forgiven so badly that I sink into his arms.

All morning, Josey's been whittling a knot of wood and watching a scene repeat itself again and again. Her grand-dad emerges from the ranch house, bare-chested and swaddled only in a towel, leading a man or woman in similar undress. The pair enters a free-standing sweat lodge made of teak. An hour later, they reappear, the client drenched and weeping, Lucas radiant and triumphant.

"He's always had people like that around." Jay takes the wood from her hand. "A unicorn?"

"A pony. It isn't done."

"When he was teaching, there was always a grad student or two living with us and a couple more at dinner every night. Acolytes. Flatters. Sycophants. *Believers.* Nothing's changed since he wrote his book. Except that they're richer and there are more of them."

"They remind me of the hippies. The ones you didn't like."

Jay strokes her hair. "Yes, they're sheep. I love you, Josey."

"I love you too, Dad."

"I'm sorry you never met your grandmother. I didn't know she was sick. You were only two. Eight years ago. She was the best of us."

Josey nestles in his lap and closes her eyes. When she wakes, her dad is gone.

There are eight of us in the riding party, or, as Lucas calls us, "the posse." The rest have paid for the privilege. I don't know the exact amount, but I'm sure it's six figures. This buys you a week on a bunk at the ranch, one-on-one sessions with Lucas, and special "self-discovery journeys" like this one.

Another perk is the playful banter, the non-stop berating. "C'mon, you city folk, stand up in them stirrups. Give those nags their head." He whips the horses and their riders into a charging frenzy.

I count a surgeon, a banker, a couple of developers, a couple of Wall Street types. Not an accomplished rider among them. And none of them ready for a hard gallop on a narrow mountain path alongside a deep gorge.

Candace, a greying woman who owns a chain of movie theaters, is in real trouble. She's lost her reins and clings to her saddle horn, her feet flying free of the stirrups. My father is nowhere. I drive my mount alongside, between her and the gorge. I'm pulling on her horse's mantle when I hear the SNAP!

Somehow I stay in my saddle. But the saddle plummets into the gorge and I plummet with it.

The ancient cat emerges from beneath the bed just before midnight. Josey strokes its coarse fur in the flickering light of a lamp. The search party returns. They stomp their cold feet, their shoulders sag and they shuffle off to bed. Her grandfather stops at her doorway only long enough to shake his head.

An older woman is there. She's one of the guests. "Would you like me to stay with you until they find your father?" Josey nods.

She is suddenly awake. Candace slumps in a stuffed chair.

She steps into the hallway, following a muffled sound. She walks silently through the darkened house, through the foyer with its collection of boots and snowshoes, through the living room decorated in hanging Navajo rugs and antlers, past the modern kitchen, venturing into an area that is clearly off limits to guests. There is a doorway there.

She peers up a steep, dark stairway. Light sneaks from the bottom of a closed door at the top.

Something is moving in there. It wheezes. It rattles. She tries the door. Locked.

No sleep. Just cold. The only thing that dawn brings to the table is light.

My right leg is twisted under me. The left is between some rocks the size of refrigerators. Both legs hurt but I won't know if they're broken until I stand up. I can't imagine that ever happening.

Yet I'm suddenly upright, staring into a very angry face. Crew-cut. Vietnam tan. I'm in his close-up. "You're Jay James. I've been looking for you. You killed my sister."

The sun crests over the cliff, the one I fell from last night, just as he knocks me to the ground again.

Sleep please.

"Don't you fear, little girl. Your father knows these mountains well. Hell, he was born in 'em. Did he ever tell you that story?"

Josey feels uncomfortable on the old man's lap. She knows the arm around her shoulder is meant to comfort and assure, but it feels stiff and unnatural. She's glad Candace is here in the study – she's glad she's not alone with her grandfather.

"Hand me down that photograph over my desk." Candace passes him the faded photo of a small cabin standing alone in a deep valley. "*Oblaye H^tayetu*

Naghi, the Hopis called it, 'The Valley Of The Evening Soul.'"

Her grandfather's eyes fix on a memory. "It was a long time ago. I was a much younger man. About your father's age. I spent an entire summer building that cabin with my own hands. It was hard work, and I was often lonely. When it was done, I was pretty proud. I brought my wife, your grandmother, to see it. Our first real home away from the city, away from the university, away from my work. A place where we could start, where we could build something. In fact, we were already expecting our first child. We were happy."

A storm seems to gather and he pauses. "That night, she went into labor. Six weeks premature. All the way out there. Miles from a doctor, miles from anywhere. All alone."

"What did you do?"

"I possessed the moment. I delivered the child myself. And that child was your father."

Josey can't help herself. She crawls from his arms into Candace's. Lucas doesn't seem to notice, still living in that distant moment.

1889

The old German man rides into town with his fat Mexican whore. Arango greets him warmly, calls him Frank and speaks to him with respect. The two men step into the ramshackle hacienda to confer in private.

Sunday offers Yanina a bowl of water and a clean cloth, but the woman only pushes them away. She really is a hideous thing, with dirty hair in her face and swollen features — she's a lump perched on two thick logs. After a few minutes, she gets bored and stomps inside. Sunday can hear a torrent of foul abuse in

Spanish and some whining assurances in German.

Arango steps out, looking taller and younger. He stares over Sunday's shoulders at the horizon. His eyes are filled with pride. "Frank is an emissary. The other ranchers want to meet. They want to organize. They want me to lead them."

"The ranchers from beyond the hills? Who cut your fences and steal your cattle?"

"They still fear me, even though my men are gone. They respect me."

A slap can be heard from inside. The German cries out in pain.

Sunday shakes her head. "You would trust a man like that? Who lets a grotesque whore treat him that way? He is no longer a man. He has given up the right to be treated like one. He cannot give respect when he has none for himself."

Arango's hand is a sudden blur. Sunday holds her cheek. Her eyes water but she will not cry out. She stares at her father until he turns away.

Without another word, he saddles his horse and follows the bickering pair out of Los Rios.

A riderless horse meets Sunday in the canyon, reins dragging through the dirt. This is when she knows she's about to see some dead cowboys.

There are a lot of them, mostly scattered among the rocks above the pass. *Vaqueros* in their best clothes. The horses wear the brands of Arango's enemies.

Frank's body lies draped over a bloody saddle near a narrow river. Yanina sits in the dirt by his side. She looks up when Sunday dismounts. Her mouth starts moving and it doesn't stop. Scattered among the obscenities and the insults are some bits of information that Sunday needs, so she lets the whore rant.

It was an ambush. It was Frank's idea. Frank fucked up. Arango is injured. He rode North.

Sunday considers Arango's stubborn pride. He won't be coming back to Los Rios. At least not alive.

Yanina spits on the dead man's bloody face. In a flash, a plan forms in Sunday's head. To wrap the howling bitch in rope and drop her in the shallow river. She knows where it comes from. From Jeff Waring. This is what he would do. He would place heavy stones on her chest one by one until she slowly drowned.

The whore is sputtering and spitting out lungs full

of water, but still cursing as she drowns. Crouching by the side of the river, Sunday remembers something else about the man who claimed to be her father for seventeen years. When all was said and done, Waring was a practical man. If he were here, he would shoot Yanina in the head and be done with her.

Sunday pries Frank's gun from his dead fingers and presses it against the whore's forehead.

Suddenly, Sunday remembers the rest. She lowers the gun.

"His blood doesn't flow in me."

Yanina sits by a warm fire. She's unbound, dressed in fresh clothes, warmed and full of food.

When she finishes her coffee, Sunday kicks her ass up and down the canyon then tosses her, whimpering, on her mule and points her towards the hills, where hopefully she won't encounter any more foolish German men and can live out the rest of her life as the miserable thing that she is.

Arango

The bottle travels around the circle. No one takes as big a pull as they would like, though their throats are dry and the whiskey tastes very good. This is a rough bunch and they don't know one another at all, having each found this fire by the railroad tracks separately. The builder of the fire is unknown as is the owner of the bottle.

"Shall I tell you the story of how the Coyote tricked the wind?"

The tension around the fire doesn't allow for a nod or a grunt of agreement so Arango just proceeds.

"Coyote was wandering in the desert and he came to a great lake. Now Coyote was lazy and didn't want walk around the lake, so he said to the Water, 'Water, why don't you move aside so that I can cross?'"

As he speaks, Arango studies his new *compadres*. Their rough hands tell him that they were laborers once. They are dirty. The kind of dirty that means sleeping without much between you and the dirt.

They share something else as well. A lack of desperation. These are men who have faced desperate times and despaired. But those times are behind them. They are beyond despair now. They live with it. In it.

Just like him.

"So this is how we got the Santa Ana winds, which still blow hot when the Wind is angry. And this is how Coyote came to die of thirst at the bottom of a lake."

Arango upends the bottle. It's empty. He's drained it.

Without a word, the men fall upon him and begin to beat him.

1947

Richard

The guard at the gate waves Richard through. Richard steers his Lincoln around the backlot of MGM Studios, through the area they call The Zoo, where they shoot the exotic jungle adventure scenes.

He's thinking about his brother. He imagines the pain that Clay must have felt during his final two weeks. The starvation, the cold, the burns, the broken bones, a gun-shot wound.

Clay was never a strong man. Never a particularly driven man, either. You wouldn't call him resilient. Yet, all this did not kill him. He did that himself.

Richard supposes it was the girl. He supposes that a father's love of his daughter is a powerful thing.

Well, Richard knows that Hate is more powerful than Love. And an Idea is more powerful than anything on this planet.

Richard has an Idea. He parks in front of a bustling soundstage. A sign reads "PRODUCER". Crew members see him and get busy. His assistant rushes up. He steps from the Zephyr, ready to tell the world.

The wooden handle plunges into the detonator. Nothing happens. The director shouts, "Cut!" Richard shouts louder, "No, again!"

The actors rein their horses in the riverbed. Are the cameras still rolling? Should they ride?

"Cut!" "No, again, AGAIN!"

The TNT sparks this time and the temporary dam explodes. The water floods the channel, catching the two dozen riders unprepared. They wash downstream, towards the already completed concrete walls of the LA River.

Lotus grips her prayer book. She closes her eyes and imagines the worst. Hooves struggle for purchase in the muddy river bottom, only to find hard cement. Limbs become tangled and break. Riders submerge and drown. Carcasses of man and beast bash against the unforgiving walls and wash inland past city buildings.

She opens her eyes and it's all true. A boot breaks the surface. A thin stream of diluted blood.

She tosses the damn book into the river. Followed by the tiny crucifix that Sister gave her on her deathbed.

"Roll! Roll! Roll!" cries the man she should have killed already.

It's day 53 on the set of "The Builders" and Richard Lawrence is no longer just the producer. He's doing everybody's job. He designed the night club and now he's rehearsing the dancers. The director whines, "The last time I saw the Apache dance was in a Clara Bow film."

The bar has been built to Richard's specifications and, at his insistence, stocked with real liquor. The grip department is drinking very good scotch from their coffee cups. They are all big, angry-looking men. Carter is the biggest and he looks the angriest.

Carter takes a long pull and glares at this manic

intrusion into his world. "The Builders" is his 110th film. He's been on a film set for most of his waking hours over the last 17 years. He started out running reels across the lot. Now he's Johnson's top man. On the next picture, he'll be key grip.

The actors are gathered in the center of the sound-stage, leads and bit-characters both, in costume and full make-up. Richard paces before them. "You actors, listen to me. Each line you deliver, each gesture, each exhalation must come from your core. It must come directly from that space inside you that determines who you are, and how you relate to the world." Richard chain smokes. He chews on a pencil between puffs. "And always remember the following. Remember as you deliver these lines of mine, remember that they *are mine*! I am paying for this entire film. The studios will line up to distribute it when I finish. But until then, it belongs to me." He spots an errant cable and coils it around and around in his hands. "Each of you is a tool which I use to tell my story. It is your nature to be a tool as it is my nature to use you. And because you are a tool, each line, each gesture, each breath you take is in service of this story I am telling. Imagine a pyramid like the pharaohs built. The shape is the story. The pinnacle is the idea. You are the stones."

Carter believes in the film-making process. He believes in the hierarchy of the set. He believes in the division of labor. He's heard enough. He balls his fists and stamps towards this asshole.

Richard pitches into the air. He lands on his back and shakes, convulsing.

Carter stops dead. He's still 10 feet away. He stares at his hands.

Lady Richard and Lotus stand on an empty sound-stage. It is cold but still smells of human sweat. A dull square of sunlight marks a distant doorway. Lotus flips switches and connects lines but all the lights have been struck. The only thing that works is the "Filming In Progress" light. It colors the two women red.

"Richard finished everything he started. It was his nature." Lady Richard's eyes scan the floor. They must be near the spot where her husband dropped. His heart officially stopped two hours later in the hospital, but she considers this the place of his death. "He left two things undone. The Golden State hotel is still under construction. And then there is this. This film. I have to finish them both."

Lotus considers the immensity of these undertakings. Lady knows as much about construction as she does about film-making. She knows less than Lotus who knows nothing. "What will you do when they are done?"

"Never think of him again."

Lotus takes her hand. "I'll help."

1949

The Cinegrill is the place to be in Hollywood on a Friday night. It's splashy and it's pricey. Lotus is treating herself. She's even booked a suite in the adjacent Roosevelt Hotel.

She can afford it. And she deserves it. Over the last two years, she has distinguished herself. She honored her promise to Lady and oversaw the final months of shooting Richard's epic film "The Builders" then cut the film herself. When no studio wanted it, she distributed the film on her own, working out deals directly with theater owners and opening the film in every major city in the country.

The other venture that Richard's death left unfinished was the Golden State Hotel. Its completion was tricky, involving a near blizzard of paper and an ocean of greased palms. She learned the names of the players in Los Angeles and just how much their cooperation cost. The Golden opened on time and under budget. This earned her the grudging respect of the all-male Board of Directors, and promotion to President of Lawrence Enterprises from Lady Richard herself.

She sips her martini, sinking into a padded leather chair at the best private table. Her eyes dance over the cinema décor of the place, following the murals on the walls of Hollywood stars, Keystone Kops, cowboys and Indians and damsels in distress. She has produced a movie. She's part of that history now.

For the first time in a long time, her mind turns to Sister Aimee. She wonders if Sister might not have had a second act, if she hadn't passed so suddenly. Sister had written a script for a film, "Clay In The Potter's Hands". Paramount shot some screen tests.

Lotus wonders where that script is. She wonders if she should option it. Second acts are important.

Pretty people surround her. The women in their

chiffon evening dresses with their shoulders bared. The men with their wide lapels and top-pleat trousers. Her own dress is a Christian Dior original. She admires how the flared skirt spreads over her crossed legs. She takes another sip of her martini.

The band is back from break. The maestro, in his perfect tuxedo, conducts from the dance floor. He is clearly a passionate and accomplished man.

Another well-dressed man steps to his side and, to Lotus' horror, *slaps* the conductor. And he *continues* to slap the man, his hands weaving through the maestro's still-conducting arms. The madness escalates! A third man appears, slapping the second. And then a fourth! It's a cacophony of swinging arms! The band plays on!

She doesn't know what to make of it. Is it revolution?

A cigarette girl appears, handing the men matching megaphones. They turn as one, revealing it was all a gag, that they are just a bunch of bouncers and heavies. They belt out operatic lyrics with thick New York accents.

The crowd roars but soon forgets. It's clearly a regular feature and they treat it as such. Disposable entertainment.

Having spent a year cutting Richard's film, she

knows his philosophy well. It's mostly crap but he got one thing right. People's natures do not change.

She quietly finishes her martini, realizing it is her last. Her last drink, her last nightclub, her last attempt at being a part of the crowd.

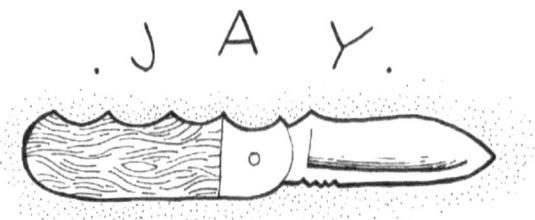

.J A Y.

1970

The bartender of the Silverlode laughs. "You're the third guy to ask about the Lucas place this week."

The big man takes off his black-rimmed glasses. He polishes the lenses on his new flannel shirt. "That the truth?"

"Last Friday, Lucas' son walks in here, wants to know the way to the ranch. Then yesterday, some young kid is asking the same question."

Walker stops polishing. "Tell me about this kid."

The kid's passion never abates. I struggle to detach.

His tools of torture so far have included a knife, a ragged rope, a tree sapling. Also, a hot metal rod, a hot fork – he uses the wood stove to heat them up.

He talks while he works on me, and he talks fast. The topics roll this way and that, mostly personal experiences, a lot of anger. Sooner or later, it all rolls around to his sister at which point the pain increases. After two days, I've got the order of the ensuing monologue down. He begins with descriptions of her beauty, of her innocence. There's a story from their youth which usually involves a family pet but sometimes is about their summer trips to the Maine coast. Then comes her corruption by guys like me. This is an especially painful hour. The pain drops for a bit as he loses himself in the narrative of his search for her. Lots of aimless wandering, he was fresh out of the corps, he didn't know where to look — he paints his reaction to specific scenes of depravity that he witnessed with the hippies and diggers. His point is to illustrate how naive he was. How ill-prepared he was. It justifies his decision to hook up with Walker. It underlines how far he's come.

It has taken days to decipher his relationship to Walker. My guess is that he's a cult-deprogrammer of some sort. The kid alternately describes him as a detective and a savior. He finds the lost children of the wealthy and removes them from the happenings and the counter-culture. He sticks them in a hotel room somewhere and starves them and yells at them for a couple weeks and delivers them to their parents, and dubs them "cured". But first he has to find them. That's where the kid comes in.

Now the bragging. How he follows the hippies. How he's figured them out. This is a light interlude, but I know the big pain is coming. That's when he finds his sister. She's dead. She's in a meadow with her throat slit and beat to hell. I did it. I'm a sick bastard. I'm going to pay.

This is where I black out. When I come to, he's weeping and muttering about the Blue Light.

It's like a light bulb flickering in a dark room. Flash, I'm conscious. Flash, all is black.

A big man is there in the cabin with the kid. They are both talking fast and I think they're talking about me and then there is darkness.

The man is wearing heavy glasses now and reading something. He looks at me and raises the book. "Your father's diary. From a summer about thirty years ago.

Interesting reading…" The kid is lying in the corner. He's looking at me too but his eyes are blank holes and it is dark again.

The man has pulled a chair closer to the wood stove. He must be Walker. The diary is cradled in his lap. He's studying some odd looking tools — corroded steel. "He used these to get you out. Out of your mother." He snorts a little, sort of in an amazed way, sort of admiring too. "He wrote it all down here. *All* of it! Even the recipe of the little cocktail he gave your mother. It's not a confession; it's like notes, notes on a procedure he's proud of. He induced your early birth. Here! In the middle of the woods with no way to get to a hospital or find a doctor. You and your mother both survived, but there was a lot of blood involved. I don't think he did it for a kick. I think he did it to see if he could pull it off. He writes something…here it is, 'to rise to the moment and master it.'"

I'm thinking how my mother is dead and how I deserve all this pain but Walker is laughing. "I want to meet this guy!"

It's just me and the kid in the cabin now, and he's not getting up. But I do and it hurts like nothing ever has. Even more than the last, what, two? three? days of torture.

I reach the door before my legs stop working. I can hear Walker's braying voice on the other side. "You have to witness the scene to really get it, to really understand these Gatherings. I'm telling you, Hippie Land is a killing field. It's the happy hunting grounds."

I inch the door open. Walker is talking to two men. One is my father.

"No one cares about these people. The police sure don't. The police aren't going to bother with an investigation if a couple of crazy hippies end up dead. They're out there in the middle of nowhere; they're outside of society *by choice*. As far as family or friends are concerned, they don't know anything. So who's going to notice when someone drops *all the way* out?"

My father interrupts. "What is your point?"

"I'm trying to help you understand your son. The temptation is too much. If you're crazy like that kid partner of mine, or you're just mean like me, or if you got some shit to work out like your son — man, the opportunity is there! Eventually, you are going take it."

I can see the other man now. It's Marks. He's holding

the reins on a pair of horses.

"Now, in the scheme of things, Jay has killed a lot less than most. Maybe two or three tops. But, it doesn't matter. I can pin a truckload of bodies on him, starting with my partner in there."

Lucas seems to be studying Walker's shirt collar. "What do you want?"

"I want in." Walker sounds hungry. "I want to be part of Blue Light."

My dad fishes something out of his pocket. He stuffs the wad carefully into his right ear. Marks pulls a shotgun from his saddle and hands it to him. Lucas walks several studied paces backwards. He raises the shotgun. He takes a deep breath and slowly lets it out.

Walker screams "wait" and covers his face. The blast takes off his fingers and most of his face.

Lucas hands the gun to Marks and walks towards me. He opens the door and I stagger on my feet.

"When was the last time you were in a canoe, son?"

Detective Evan Blackford studies the case file on Phoebe James. He's amazed. The Saratoga police actually gave a shit about this one. They got fingerprints off the girl's necklace, some silver Indian thing. They matched them to their man and even found the murder weapon on him.

It takes him a few minutes to place the killer — it's *Jessup*, the undercover hippie cop. Real name: John Mackey. They used to yuck it up about that show back at the Academy. He shuffles the photo to the side of his desk, studies the arresting officer's notes. Looks like Mackey's been playing a different role in real life, some sort of guru, calls himself the "Magic Man", got a little following. Must have been fun. Now he's going to prison for a long time.

He reaches for the phone. Then he remembers he doesn't know how to reach Jay. "Well," he thinks, "he'll be relieved when he hears the news."

My father watches Walker's body sink below the canoe. He pulls the kid's corpse closer and grabs some rope. "You alive?"

I'm basically dead. Even hopped up on adrenaline, I can barely grunt.

"You're next, son. " He methodically ties heavy rocks to the corpse. He takes his time. He's always been proud of his knotting. "It's not because of the trouble you brought here. These bodies will be underwater for a long time. Marks is cleaning up the rest. It's because of my plans for the future. You wouldn't be comfortable there."

The kid slides into the lake. His army-issue boots are the last thing under. Lucas starts working on my legs.

"Your friend down there, Walker, he was nuts. But he's just part of the natural progression of things. That's what the prophets of your era don't understand. They don't realize that a movement based on complete freedom can only lead to one of two outcomes. Either crime or commerce. I choose the latter."

I struggle but he holds me until the strength passes out of me again. He resumes securing the heavy weights to my body and I resume watching.

"A successful prophet knows that you have to keep raising the bar. Jesus understood this. Escalation, Jay. Water to wine, giving sight to the blind, raising the dead — building the miracles one after another until the big finale, his own resurrection. Cheating death! That is success, son."

This sudden passion gives me the spark to speak. "What is Blue Light?"

His eyes flash and he swings an oar. An explosion of

pain and I'm in the water.

I hear a scream and see someone on a bluff high above the lake. It's Josey, staring down. Her mouth is a circle. I sink.

When Josey reaches the ranch, she's stumbling like she's blind. She can still see her father sinking into the river, his face turned up towards her. This image is superimposed over everything in front of her eyes. A double-exposure like how they make ghosts appear in scary movies.

She rushes through the house, throwing open doors, searching for a human face to replace the horrible vision that haunts her. She finds no one. The place is deserted. She runs outside and collapses. The sobs come now. And the horrible shaking.

She feels a hand softly stroke her hair. It's the older woman, the one who held her last night when she was afraid. "Lucas sent everyone away. The staff too. Everyone."

Josey stares hard, forcing the kind face to fill her entire field of vision. She grabs air between sobs. "He killed my dad."

Candace takes her hand and they walk briskly away from the ranch. The sun is setting fast. Candace knows there's a barn out there somewhere in the gathering darkness but she doesn't like the idea of dragging Josey around looking for it. The only shelter she can see is the teak sweat lodge Lucas uses for his vision quests. They huddle inside.

When Josey can breathe again, she asks, "Why didn't you go with them?"

"Do you know what my name means? It's from the bible. Candace means Queen of Children, after a woman who protected children. That's why I chose it. I know all about fathers. Children need protecting."

Her words calm Josey. "What was your old name?"

"The name the church gave me. Lotus."

Critter is in the tractor's cab. He'll probably spend the night there. Earlier, he woke up in his cot, drenched in piss. That's been happening more and more lately, especially when he's up late drinking. It's so damn cold. That cot won't dry for hours. Better to sleep in the tractor.

He's finishing the bottle when something moves

over by the door. He peers into the darkness of the barn. There's something stirring near the hayloft now, something big. He snaps on the headlights.

A man is standing there, covered head to foot in mud. He opens his fist. "I need the keys to the pump."

Critter stares. It's the owner's son. He looks like wet death. Critter hands him all the keys. Jay staggers outside.

He tries to stay awake but it's too much. The rhythmic glub glub of the pumps, the splash of gasoline in a bucket, Jay rustling off and returning to glub glub and splash again. He drifts off.

When he wakes, Jay is standing there with a torch. Critter decides to tell him a story.

"This land had a lot of different uses before your dad came along. Indians used to make camp here. I've seen pieces of their pots and such. There was a pretty big silver mine not too far from here. It's long gone now. Folks used to come up here to fish and hunt. I'd show them around some, made my living that way for a long time. It's my home and I knew I'd see it change. But I never thought I'd see anything like your father and his group of crazies. It surprises the hell out me. I betcha the land is pretty surprised too."

Jay hands him a torch. "Fix things."

Critter opens a battered wooden box he keeps under the seat. He hands Jay an old pistol. "You too."

The night is deep black with only the hint of a moon hiding somewhere in the wilderness. Guests aren't allowed their own cars up here so Candace and Josey aren't going anywhere until morning's light. Without a plan, they huddle close in the cold sweat lodge and wait.

Josey shuts her eyes tight, wraps her arms around her knees and pushes at the image of her drowning father, trying to force it out of her head. Candace knows she has to start talking before the girl slips further away.

"Do you like movies, Josey?" The girl nods slightly. "I made one once. I finished it for someone. No one wanted to show it so I ended up buying the theaters. Now I own a chain." Candace closes her own eyes. "In the movie, there is an ancient race called The Builders. Long ago, these beings gave Man all he needed to create a perfect society — will, intellect, individuality. The Builders check in on Mankind from time to time to gauge their progress. In the film, they visit us three times in our history. Each time, the world is a mess ruled by a senseless mob. And each time, there exists a single guardian of these sacred truths — a sole visionary who keeps the flame alive but at the cost of his own life. The film ends in the future, where these martyred visionaries have triumphed and Mankind has realized its full potential."

It seems to be working. Josey stops rocking. Her eyes are open.

"The film is full of bad ideas. I've rejected them all as I rejected the man who wrote it. But, somehow, I've continued to hope for a Utopian future. I think that's why I was so ready to believe in Lucas James and his vision of our world. This mountain was my utopia. I fell in love with everything about it. I've spent months in libraries and classrooms, studying everything I could find about this land and the people who lived here…"

They listen. It sounds like someone is moving around in the ranch house. Josey closes her eyes again. Candace lowers her voice and leans close.

"But that's a boring story. Let me tell you a good one. Let me tell you the story of Sunday Waring."

1889

When the wagon pulls up to the Assayer's office, Arango starts lighting fuses. A half-dozen men with rifles flank the building, scanning the crowded street. Two more with pistols on their belts begin unloading bags of silver.

Arango counts five of his men traversing the muddy street. There are five more on horseback somewhere nearby. They blend in well with the miners who've come to town to blow their wages. A few months earlier, they would have joined them, drinking and screwing and maybe springing for a bath to wash away the grime. That was before the owners brought in thugs from Denver to break heads and quash any talk of unions. When wages were cut to fifty-cents a day, some grumbled and some complained and those that shouted were driven by gunpoint to the edge of town.

When Arango stumbled upon their camp, they were making periodic raids and hauling off mining supplies — shovels, picks, blasting caps, dynamite. They were also starving. Arango taught them to take their revenge in a more lucrative manner.

The building explodes in a hail-storm of splintered timber. The guards stagger aimlessly through smoke and falling debris, left dazed and deaf from the blast.

Arango's men only have to shoot a few. They rise from the street or swoop in on their horses and, as Arango's second blast blows a wall off the saloon, they commandeer the wagon and ride hell-bent for the mountains.

Arango catches up with them as they enter the trees. He sees pride on their faces even as they ride for their lives. After taking that beating at the tracks, Arango has wanted only one thing. It took a lot of work to gain the trust of these desperate men. Now he has what he's been looking for. Respect.

He throws a glance over his shoulder. The army

patrol has left town at a full gallop. It won't be long until the soldiers catch them.

Captain Hudson pushes his steed hard over rough ground. The wagon won't last much longer in this terrain. He makes the signal to bear arms.

The patrol crests a bluff and enters a large clearing. The wagon stands deserted. The outlaws' horses mill about, empty saddles. Hudson circles the wagon. Where are the men? There is no cover for hundreds of yards. The soldiers pull up hard, scattered, looking to him for an order.

Brockson opens his mouth to shout when suddenly the patrol is surrounded by men. They have appeared from thin air, armed to the teeth.

Arango raises his pistol. "It all ends here at *Caballo Blanco*."

Arango's army is on the run again. This time they hit the mine at Leadville. They made off with a sack of cash and only caught a few bullets. But the posse was ready this time, and formidable. A couple dozen armed and angry riders are hot on their trail.

Arango charges over the bluff and into the clearing they call *Caballo Blanco*, dismounting from his horse at a run. He lets go of the reins and drops into the closest hole. The rest of the men disappear underground as well, their steeds wandering off to chew on tall grass.

Arrango leans against the strong dirt wall. He and his band of former miners dug them all, an interlacing matrix of tunnels running under the entire field, with multiple entrances and exits. They also dug holes for their many pursuers, nearly a hundred graves now.

He readies his gun. Through the earth, he feels the thunder of the posse's horses. He can hear the clatter of sharply reined mounts. He can hear shouts of confusion. He prepares to leap out. This is the signal. His men will follow.

From behind him in the dark, someone grabs his arm.

It's Sunday.

. J A Y .

1970

The door to the ranch house hangs open. It's dark in there. Has Lucas returned from the lake? If he has, I'm going to find him and I'm going to kill him.

I raise the old pistol and follow it inside. My bare feet navigate the furniture and loose rugs. The only sound is the slog of my wet clothes. I stop moving and listen.

At first I think I'm hearing my own breathing. It's a ragged wheezing sound. I get a fix on it. It's coming from the kitchen. It's coming from behind a door in the back of a closet. Why is there a door there?

Behind the door is a dark stairway and at the top of those stairs there is another door. White light peeks from under it. I climb the stairs. The wheezing is now accompanied by a small beep. I push the door open.

A figure lies on a hospital bed in a white room. The wheezing is from the ventilator that keeps her breathing. The beeping is from the machine that monitors her vital functions. There are other sounds now and other machines whose duties I don't know.

But I know the woman on the bed. It's my mother.

Candace grips Josey's hand tight as they run. She can see the beam of Lucas' flashlight behind them. He's moving at the slow, steady rate of a man confident in his abilities in the woods. His prey is a middle-aged city-dweller and a young girl. Having flushed them from their hiding place, he knows it won't be long until he catches them. Candace knows this as well.

A sliver of moonlight gives her a wink through the thick trees. It renews her hope and she pushes Josey on.

They enter the clearing and she searches the darkness at their feet, a prayer repeating and drumming in her ears. "Our father who art in heaven, hallowed be thy name…" There it is! She is swallowed by the earth, pulling Josey with her.

They huddle close in the darkness of the tunnel, pressing their bodies to the damp earth. Above them, they can hear Lucas searching.

Josey's breathing is sharp and jagged. "Finish the story. Please."

Candace whispers. "After Sunday left the Yanina woman, she pointed her horse North. She started riding and she didn't quit. She rode for days and weeks and months. Somewhere on the trail she met up with the preacher called David. He had never stopped looking for her. He showed her a wanted poster of her father. After that, they rode together. They holed up in an abandoned Pony Express post near Berthoud Falls for a long time. They'd ride in one direction and then return. The next day, they'd pick another direction. Each time they rode longer and further. Finally, Sunday found Arango. At his hide-out. Right here in *Caballo Blanco*."

Candace hears the thud of Lucas' boots above them. He's close. Josey is shaking. Candace pulls her closer, whispering into her ear.

"When Arango saw her, everything changed. She had forgiven him, you see. Arango quit outlawing and returned to Los Rios where he spent the rest of his life working to restore the hacienda to its former glory. Each day, he would rise at dawn and work until dark. He only took three days off before he died, and those were on the days that his grandchildren were born. Three girls."

They hear a bellow and some crashing as Lucas charges back into the woods.

Josey begins to cry. "A happy ending…"

The ranch house must be burning pretty good by now, judging by how fast Lucas charges up the stairs. I'm sitting bedside, holding Mom's hand and the pistol.

He just stands there for awhile. "It broke my heart when you didn't come to your mother's funeral."

"What heart? Last I heard, Mom was on life support and you turned off the machines. But you never did. Resurrection? Was that the idea?"

He smooths the sheets. "Yes, but I waited too long. The drugs I've used to maintain the coma have diminished your mother. I'm afraid she's really gone now."

"That would have been quite a trick."

"It sure has captured some folks' attention. For years now, there have been rumors and whispers that I have the secret, that I possess the power to restore life. I don't discourage them." He stares fondly at his wife. "The Blue Light Project. Where do they come up with these names?"

Flames lick at the door. Smoke is filling the room. "You're not going to shoot me."

"I won't have to."

"Then we all die together."

"Like a family."

Dawn is breaking over the mountains as Candace and Josey emerge from the earth. The ranch house is a smoldering black frame. Ash floats around the woman and the girl as they walk in a dream towards the sun.

Candace starts Critter's truck. The engine coughs to life along with the radio. It emits a constant static. She begins to cry.

Josey takes her hand and holds it tight.

Together, they begin their journey down the mountain road. As they approach town, they pick up a signal. Clear as a bell, a gospel choir sings a hymn from Candace's youth.

> Just a closer walk with Thee,
> Grant it, Jesus, is my plea,
> Daily walking close to Thee,
> Let it be, dear Lord, let it be.

1901

The baby room is much brighter than when Sunday first saw it, twelve years before. The mural now circles the walls. It tells her story, but it also tells of the birth of three children and how they've grown. She can hear them now, outside the hacienda, laughing and playing with her husband.

She steps outside to join them, her beautiful daughters and the good man who is their father.

BURNT originally appeared on-line in serial form. Chapters were published weekly between January 2010 and February 2011.

ABOUT THE AUTHOR

Tim Kirk is a writer and filmmaker. Among his films are *Room 237*, *The Nightmare* and *Director's Commentary: Terror of Frankenstein*. He lives in Los Angeles and is proud to produce *Tom Explores Los Angeles* and to have written the narration for the "Hall of The Crucifixion" presentation at Forest Lawn – Glendale.